To BUY
from K-town
: Rice, yakult,
spring onion

K-TOWN

FOR MOM
& DAD

First Edition

1 3 5 7 9 10 8 6 4 2

Library of Congress Cataloging-in-Publication Data

Names: Kim, Aram, author, illustrator.

Title: Sunday funday in Koreatown / Aram Kim.

Description: First edition. | New York : Holiday House, [2021]

Series: Yoomi, friends, and family | Audience: Ages 3–7. | Audience: Grades K–1.

Summary: Every Sunday, Yoomi enjoys favorite foods and activities
in Koreatown but when things go wrong, Daddy encourages
her to try new things and she still has a wonderful day.

Identifiers: LCCN 2020016046 | ISBN 9780823444472 (hardcover)

Subjects: CYAC: Koreatowns—Fiction. | Resilience (Personality trait)—Fiction.

Korean Americans—Fiction. | Fathers and daughters—Fiction.

Classification: LCC PZ7.1.K55 Sun 2021 | DDC [E]—dc23

LC record available at https://lccn.loc.gov/2020016046

Sunday Funday in Koreatown

ARAM KIM

HOLIDAY HOUSE · NEW YORK

Sunday is Funday!
Yoomi wakes up to watch her favorite TV show.

On Sundays, Dad helps Yoomi make anything she wants for breakfast.

But not today.
"We ran out of rice," says Dad.

Yoomi eats cereal.

Yoomi gets ready. She's going to wear her favorite shirt!

"It will dry tomorrow," says Mom.
"But tomorrow isn't Funday," says Yoomi.

Mom helps Yoomi put on her second-favorite shirt.

On Sundays, Yoomi and Dad ride the bus to . . .

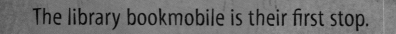

The library bookmobile is their first stop.

Yoomi wants to read the Korean folktale about the grandma and the tiger.
"That book is already checked out," says Ms. Rah.

"This book is good, too."

Next stop is the Korean grocery store where they have everything!

In the bakery, only one hot dog twist is left.

"Hurry, Dad!" Yoomi says.

Oh, no!

"Mmm . . . crunchy."

"That was my favorite," says Yoomi.
"Sunday Funday is NOT going well."

Dad orders patbingsoo.

"Yummy!" says Yoomi.

After the patbingsoo, Yoomi
and Dad keep shopping.
"Try some tteokbokki,
your brothers' favorite,"
says Dad.

남녀노소 모두가 즐기는 맛있는 떡볶이!

Oh, no!

"Sunday Funday is ruined," says Yoomi.
"Not so," says Dad. "It isn't finished yet.
We're going to visit Grandma."

But when Yoomi rings the bell, no one answers.

She rings again.

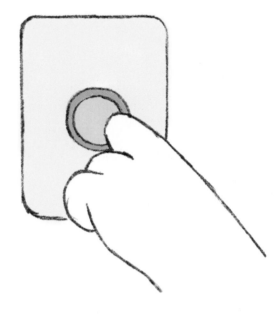

No one.

"Today is not a Funday."

Then . . .

...there is Grandma!

Grandma's sweater is the
perfect dress for Yoomi.

The book Ms.Rah
recommended is so fun!

And now they make kimbap!

What's not to love about Sunday Funday?

KOREATOWN, or K-Town, is an ethnic Korean enclave in many big cities around the world. Sometimes it comprises only a couple of blocks and sometimes it stretches out as big as a small town itself. Whatever the size, Koreatown always has many kinds of delicious Korean food, groceries with all kinds of Korean ingredients and home goods, acupuncturists, Norae-bang (aka karaoke), Korean-style spas, and a lot more!

On the second floor of the K-town in this book is a manwhabang (Comics Room), one of my favorite places to visit when I go back to Korea. In manwhabang, you can comfortably sit for hours to read stacks of comic books you love and even order snacks. If you have a Koreatown nearby, I hope you visit and explore! I'm sure you can find a favorite treat there.

KIMBAP is sticky rice and many other ingredients rolled together in toasted seaweed. It's most popular as a picnic food and as a quick bite on the go because it is easy to eat, nutritious, and yummy! When students go on field trips in Korea, everyone brings packed kimbap from home. Though basic ingredients are similar, every family has its own recipe, and it is a lot of fun to exchange kimbap with friends. Below is how my family makes kimbap.

Ingredients (serves 2)

4 cups of cooked rice

3 Tbspn vinegar

1 Tbspn sugar

1 Tsp salt

4 sheets of gim (dried seaweed sheets, both sides roasted slightly in a non-greasy pan)

4 sticks of cooked ham/sausage cut into long strips

2-4 crab sticks cut in half

2 large eggs, beaten with a pinch of salt, cooked as a rolled omelette, cut into 4 long strips

1/2 carrot cut into thirds, julienned, parboiled

1 cucumber, both ends trimmed, cut into thirds, sliced into thin strips, seeds removed

Directions

1. Over the freshly cooked rice, sprinkle vinegar, sugar, and salt, and stir well.

2. Place a sheet of gim, with the shiny side down, on a bamboo mat.

3. Spread seasoned rice evenly and thinly on the gim to 2/3 length of it (leaving about 2 inches uncovered—easier if done with gloved hand).

4. Place a stick of ham, 1 or 2 sticks of crab, a strip of egg, and a few strips of carrot and cucumber in the center of rice.

5. Roll the gim and rice over the fillings and continue rolling to the end.

6. Press the roll firmly so that the fillings are held tightly. Remove kimbap from the mat.

7. Cut the roll into bite-size pieces. Repeat with the remaining ingredients.

Visit AramKim.com, to find out more about the Koreatown pages and for translations of Korean words.